Polite Elephant

By Richard Scarry

A GOLDEN BOOK · NEW YORK

Western Publishing Company, Inc.

Racine, Wisconsin 53404

ISBN 0-307-10156-8   B C D E F G H I J

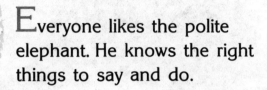

Everyone likes the polite elephant. He knows the right things to say and do.

He tips his hat and says "Hello" when he sees his friends.

When the polite elephant waits for the bus, he takes his place in line. He never pushes or shoves.

Sometimes the bus is crowded.

The polite elephant always offers his seat to a lady.

Sometimes the polite elephant goes visiting. When someone comes to the door, he tips his hat and says "Hello, Mrs. Smith. How are you?"

The polite elephant is a good guest.
He knows that some rooms are for
sitting . . . and others are for playing.

When it's time for the polite elephant to go home, he remembers to thank his friends.

"Thank you," he says. "I've had a nice time."

The polite elephant is polite at home, too. He always washes his hands and face before sitting at the table.

He sits straight in his chair. When he wants something, he says "Please." When he gets it, he says "Thank you."

Sometimes the polite elephant's friends come to his house. He greets them at the door. "Hello," he says. "Please come in."

He introduces them to his mother.
"Mommy, this is Jimmy."

The polite elephant is a good
playmate. He shares his toys with his
friends. And he is very careful when he
plays with someone else's toys.

When his friends leave, the
polite elephant goes to the door
with them. "Thank you for coming,"
he says.

The polite elephant always tries to help others in every way he can.

If you should ever meet the polite elephant, he'll be just as polite to you. He'll tip his hat and say "How do you do?"